Put Beginning Readers on the Right Track with ALL ABOARD READING™

The All Aboard Reading series is especially designed for beginning readers. Written by noted authors and illustrated in full color, these are books that children really want to read—books to excite their imagination, expand their interests, make them laugh, and support their feelings. With fiction and nonfiction stories that are high interest and curriculum-related, All Aboard Reading books offer something for every young reader. And with four different reading levels, the All Aboard Reading series lets you choose which books are most appropriate for your children and their growing abilities.

Picture Readers
Picture Readers have super-simple texts, with many nouns appearing as rebus pictures. At the end of each book are 24 flash cards—on one side is a rebus picture; on the other side is the written-out word.

Station Stop 1
Station Stop 1 books are best for children who have just begun to read. Simple words and big type make these early reading experiences more comfortable. Picture clues help children to figure out the words on the page. Lots of repetition throughout the text helps children to predict the next word or phrase—an essential step in developing word recognition.

Station Stop 2
Station Stop 2 books are written specifically for children who are reading with help. Short sentences make it easier for early readers to understand what they are reading. Simple plots and simple dialogue help children with reading comprehension.

Station Stop 3
Station Stop 3 books are perfect for children who are reading alone. With longer text and harder words, these books appeal to children who have mastered basic reading skills. More complex stories captivate children who are ready for more challenging books.

In addition to All Aboard Reading books, look for All Aboard Math Readers™ (fiction stories that teach math concepts children are learning in school); All Aboard Science Readers™ (nonfiction books that explore the most fascinating science topics in age-appropriate language); All Aboard Poetry Readers™ (funny, rhyming poems for readers of all levels); and All Aboard Mystery Readers™ (puzzling tales where children piece together evidence with the characters).

All Aboard for happy reading!

GROSSET & DUNLAP
Published by the Penguin Group
Penguin Group (USA) Inc., 375 Hudson Street, New York, New York 10014, USA
Penguin Group (Canada), 90 Eglinton Avenue East, Suite 700, Toronto,
Ontario M4P 2Y3, Canada (a division of Pearson Penguin Canada Inc.)
Penguin Books Ltd., 80 Strand, London WC2R 0RL, England
Penguin Group Ireland, 25 St. Stephen's Green, Dublin 2, Ireland
(a division of Penguin Books Ltd.)
Penguin Group (Australia), 250 Camberwell Road, Camberwell, Victoria 3124,
Australia (a division of Pearson Australia Group Pty. Ltd.)
Penguin Books India Pvt. Ltd., 11 Community Centre, Panchsheel Park,
New Delhi—110 017, India
Penguin Group (NZ), 67 Apollo Drive, Rosedale, North Shore 0632, New Zealand
(a division of Pearson New Zealand Ltd.)
Penguin Books (South Africa) (Pty.) Ltd., 24 Sturdee Avenue,
Rosebank, Johannesburg 2196, South Africa

Penguin Books Ltd., Registered Offices: 80 Strand, London WC2R 0RL, England

The publisher does not have any control over and does not assume
any responsibility for author or third-party websites or their content.

Library of Congress Cataloging-in-Publication Data is available.

Paperback ISBN 978-0-448-45241-8   10 9 8 7 6 5 4 3 2 1
Hardcover ISBN 978-0-448-45242-5   10 9 8 7 6 5 4 3 2 1

George and the Dragon

Based on the television series *Super WHY!*,
created by Angela C. Santomero, as seen on PBS KIDS

Text based on the script written by Sheila Dinsmore.

Adapted by Ellie O'Ryan   Cover Illustration by MJ Illustrations

Grosset & Dunlap

One day in Storybrook Village, Whyatt gets an important message on his Super-Duper Computer. "Looks like Pig needs our help," he says.

Pig tells Whyatt,
"Look! The giant stepped
on my new toy.
He is big and scary!
I want to get my toy back,
but I am afraid!"

Whyatt says,

"This is a super-big problem.
And a super-big problem
needs us, the Super Readers.
Calling all Super Readers!
To the Book Club!"

Whyatt, Pig, Red Riding Hood,
and Princess Pea meet
at the Book Club.
Whyatt says, "Together we will
solve Pig's problem."

Pig says, "The giant stepped on my toy. And I am scared to get it back! What can I do?"

Whyatt says,

"When we have a problem,

we look in a book!"

Princess Pea waves
her magic wand.
She says,
"Peas and carrots,
carrots and peas,
book come out,
please, please, please!"

A book flies off the shelf.
The title is
George and the Dragon.

Whyatt says,
"We need to jump into
this book to find the answer
to Pig's question.
It's time to transform!"

In a flash of stars,
the Super Readers
change into
super heroes.

They climb into their

Why Flyers and say,

"Super Readers . . . to the rescue!"

Then they fly into the book.

Princess Presto says,
"Presto! We're in the
George and the Dragon
book!"

Super Why says, "This book
is about Knight George.
He wants to rescue
Princess Hope from a tower.
But he is afraid.
A scary dragon is
keeping her there."

Princess Hope was stuck in
a tower because of a scary
dragon.

George was scared of the dragon.

Alpha Pig says,
"That's just like my problem.
I am scared of the giant,
just like George is scared
of the dragon.
We need to find George!"

The Super Readers find George.
Alpha Pig asks,
"Are you going to battle
the scary dragon?"

George says, "Yes, I am!
But I do not know
where the dragon is.
How will I find the dragon?"
asks George.

Alpha Pig says, "With my Amazing Alphabet Tools, I can find the letters in the word <u>dragon</u> so we can get to the dragon."

Alpha Pig says,

"Look! I see the letters

D-R-A-G-O-N.

That spells <u>dragon</u>.

The dragon must be

behind those trees!"

"ROAR!" goes the dragon.

"Lickety Letters!

We found the dragon!

He is very big

and very scary,"

says Alpha Pig.

"Princess Hope,
I will rescue you!"
yells George.
"ROAR!" goes the dragon.
"Ahhh!" cries George.
He is scared.

Princess Hope has an idea.
"If only we could make
the dragon fall asleep.
Then George could
get past the dragon!"

Princess Presto . . . to the rescue!

Princess Presto waves her
Magic Spelling Wand and says,
"I can spell the word <u>sleep</u>.
That will make the dragon sleep.
S-L-E-E-P. Presto!"
The dragon yawns . . .
and falls asleep.

One by one, everyone
tiptoes past the dragon.

They are trying to be very quiet.

"Shhhhh!" whispers Princess Presto.

They sneak past the dragon.

George cheers, "Hurray!"

The dragon wakes up.

"ROAR!"

George is scared.

Princess Hope says,

"Don't be scared, George!"

George says,

"But dragons scare me!

My story says so. See?

What can I do?"

The dragon scares George.

Super Why . . .
to the rescue!

Super Why says,
"I can change this story
and save the day!"
He changes the sentence.
He switches the words
<u>George</u> and <u>the dragon</u>.
Zzzzap!

George scares the dragon.

George scares the dragon.

The new sentence says,

"George scares the dragon."

George yells,

"Boogely boogely boo!"

The dragon is scared.

He stops roaring.

Princess Hope says,
"Now you don't have
to be scared, George.
Just talk to the dragon."

George says, "Dragon,
let Princess Hope
out of the tower!"
And the dragon
goes away!

Princess Hope comes
down from the tower.
She says,
"Great job, George!"

George says, "Thank you
for helping me be brave."
Princess Hope says,
"You are welcome."

Super Why says,

"It's time for us to go.

Good-bye, George.

Good-bye, Princess."

The Super Readers hop
into their Why Flyers.
They fly out of the story
and back to the Book Club.

Pig says, "Now I know
what I have to do.
I have to be brave—
just like George was brave!"

Pig runs to the park.

He says, "Excuse me, Giant.

You are standing on my toy.

May I please have it back?"

The giant says, "I am sorry!
I did not mean to step on your toy!"
He gives the toy back to Pig.

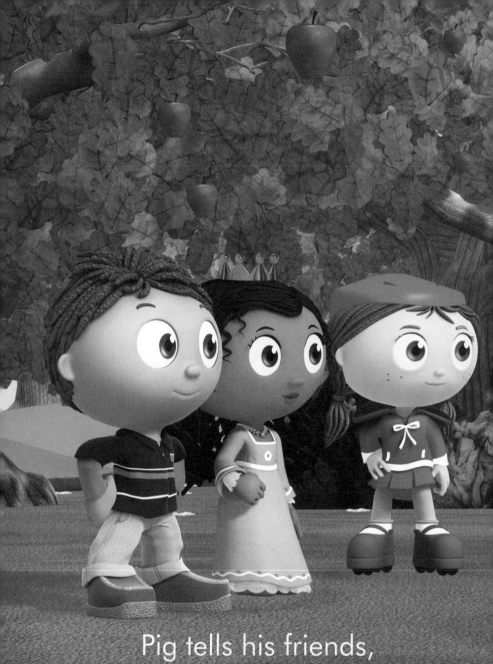

Pig tells his friends,
"I was so brave.
I got my toy back
from the giant!"

"Way to go, Pig!"
everyone cheers.

"Hip, hip, hurray! The Super Readers saved the day!
We changed the story. We solved the problem.
We worked together so . . .
Hip, hip, hurray! The Super Readers saved the day!"